June Morley, winner of
The Works Bedtime
Reading Event

"I was thrilled to win the Bedtime
Story competition. The experience
of having my book published is
an exciting bonus."

For Adam, Lee and Anneka,
J. M.

For Charlie.
Love, B. G.

First published 2009 by Walker Books Ltd
87 Vauxhall Walk, London SE11 5HJ

2 4 6 8 10 9 7 5 3 1

Text © 2009 June Morley
Illustrations © 2009 Brita Granström

The moral rights of June Morley and Brita Granström to be identified as
author and illustrator respectively have been asserted.

This book has been typeset in Colwell Roman

Printed in China

British Library Cataloguing in Publication Data:
a catalogue record for this book is available from the British Library

ISBN 978-1-4068-1616-2

www.walker.co.uk

# LITTLE MOLE
## AND THE
# FADING SUN

June Morley

Illustrated by Brita Granström

WALKER BOOKS
AND SUBSIDIARIES

LONDON • BOSTON • SYDNEY • AUCKLAND

Little Mole went out to play.
"Be home before the sun fades away,"
said Mummy Mole, "and keep close to
the molehills so you don't get lost."

Little Mole made lots of new hills

and played roly-poly all day long.

Then the wood began to get dark.
"Oh, no," cried Little Mole, "the sun
is fading. But which way is home?"

Maybe this way? he thought.
So off he went, following the fading
sun until he was too tired to go on.

Just then, Hedgehog peeped out
from a pile of leaves.
"What's wrong?" she asked.
"I must be home before the sun
fades away," said Little Mole.

"Climb onto my back," said
Hedgehog, "and I'll carry you."

So Hedgehog and Little Mole followed
the fading sun until Hedgehog was
too tired to go on.

Badger popped out from behind
a tree.
"What's wrong?" he asked.
"Little Mole must be home before
the sun fades away," said Hedgehog.

"Climb onto my back," said Badger,
"and I'll carry you both."

So Badger, Hedgehog
and Little Mole
followed the fading
sun until Badger was
too tired to go on.

Horse stopped eating the grass and looked up. "What's wrong?" she asked. "Little Mole must be home before the sun fades away," said Badger.

"Climb onto my back," said Horse, "and I'll carry you all."

So Horse, Badger, Hedgehog and
Little Mole followed the
fading sun until ...

# BUZZZZ ...

a bee landed on Horse's nose.

"AACHOO!" sneezed Horse, sending Badger, Hedgehog and Little Mole tumbling to the ground. AACHOO!

Suddenly, Little Mole was rolling
down a long, dark tunnel. Then ...

# BUMP!

he landed on a
soft, warm
bed of
earth.

"Just in time," said
Mummy Mole.

The sun faded away
and Little Mole fell
sound asleep.

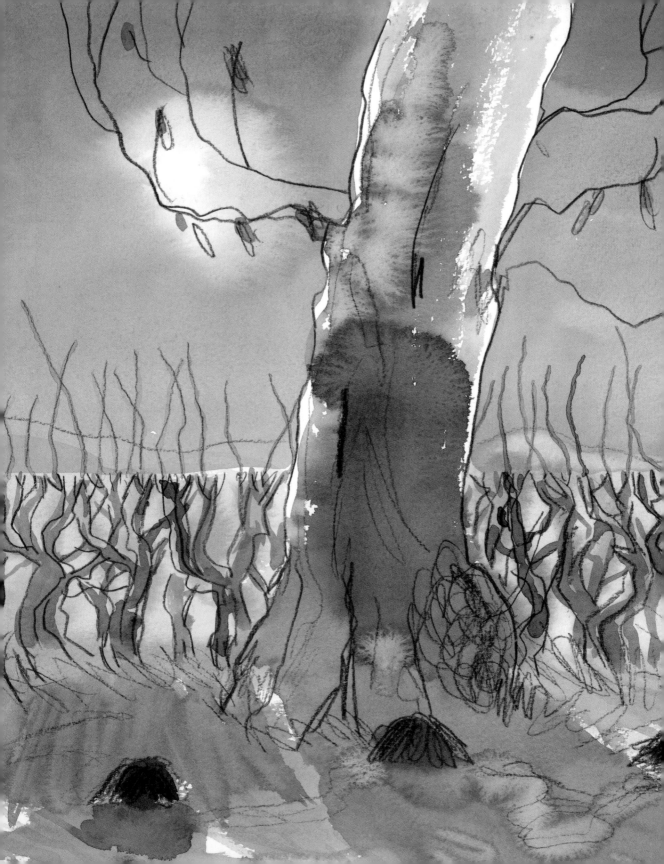